THE
NEW PUPPY
FROM THE
BLACK LAGOON®

THE
NEW PUPPY
FROM THE
BLACK LAGOON®

by Mike Thaler
Illustrated by Jared Lee

SCHOLASTIC INC.

For Laurel, John & Grace Cairney
—M.T.

To my little buddy, Skipper
—J.L.

IGUANA

TREAT

Text Copyright © 2017 by Mike Thaler
Illustrations Copyright © 2017 by Jared Lee

ISBN 978-1-338-24461-8

10 9 8 7 6 5 4 3 2   17 18 19 20 21

Printed in the U.S.A.   40
First printing 2017

from BONE

TREAT

PARROT

CONTENTS

TREAT

CHAPTER 1
ANTICIPATION

There was a time when I didn't have a dog, but there was never a time when I didn't want one.

I'D LIKE TO HAVE A DOG.

YOU'LL HAVE TO ASK YOUR MOM.

After years of begging, Mom finally gives in and says I can get a puppy.

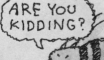

DO YOU HAVE ANY BUG SPRAY?

ARE YOU KIDDING?

There are so many different kinds of dogs. I need to do some research.

There are Poodles, Doodles, and Schnoodles.

There are Schnauzers, Bowsers, and Beagles.

There are big dogs and little dogs.

There are hairless dogs and hairy dogs.

There are water dogs, herding
dogs, and hunting dogs.

I go to the school library and ask Mrs. Beamster for a book on all the dog breeds.

I look at every picture. I can't make up my mind.

11

If I get a Dalmation, I could ride on a fire engine.

← FIREBUG

If I get a Saint Bernard, he could save me in a blizzard.

SNOWBIRD ⟶

If I get a Bloodhound, I'd never get lost.

HAPPY DOG

14

Mom says I will know my dog when I see it.

CHAPTER 2
MAKING MY HEART POUND

The next day, we drive to the pound. The dogs all start to bark when we walk in.

As I go from cage to cage, they all look at me with big, sad eyes.

Choose me, choose me! Take me home . . . please! they all plead.

Then I see him. A little white puppy with two black ears and a wagging tail. Actually, it's wagging so fast—it's spinning. That's it! Love at first sight.

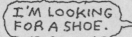

CHAPTER 3
GETTING TO KNOW YOU

I hold the puppy in my lap all the way home. He wants to look at everything all at once.

19

It is like he is seeing the world for the first time, and so am I. Everything is new.

As he licks my face, I ask Mom, "What should I call him?"

"What do you like best about him?" Mom asks.

"He's very eager, Mom—we could call him 'Egor.' He's also very friendly. We could call him 'Buddy.' But best of all, I like the way his tail spins. Let's call him 'Tailspin.'"

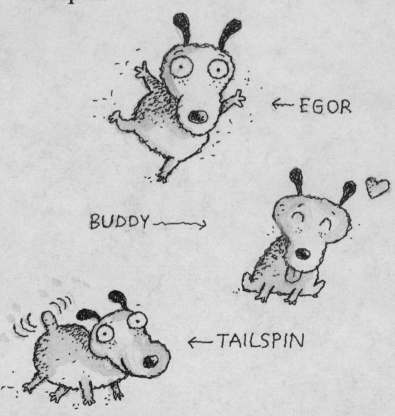

← EGOR

BUDDY ⟶

← TAILSPIN

CHAPTER 4
A MIND OF HIS OWN

When we get home, Tailspin explores every corner of our house. Mom puts down a little blanket and a bowl of water in the corner of the laundry room and tells him this is his place.

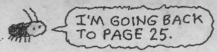 I'M GOING BACK TO PAGE 25.

Then she says, "Stay," but Tailspin has other ideas.

Mom says it will be my job to train him. Also, I will have to take him for walks, bathe him, and take him to the bathroom.

SLOW DOWN.

DON'T JUMP OUT.

GET A LITTLE CLOSER.

I tell Tailspin to sit and stay—
but he just wants to run and play.

CHAPTER 5

HOME IS WHERE THE HEART IS

That night at bedtime, Mom puts Tailspin on his blanket and closes the laundry room door. But he immediately starts to whine. Mom says he'll stop after a little while, but he doesn't.

His howl echoes through my heart.

After an hour, I go to the laundry room, pick him up, hug him, and bring him to my bed, where he immediately falls asleep.

CHAPTER 6
PARTY POOPER

The next morning, Tailspin wakes up before I do.

By the time I get up, he's long gone. Mom comes into my room. She leads me into the living room. There in the middle of the rug is a little brown pile.

"Hubie, you are going to have to train Tailspin so these accidents don't keep happening."

"I'm on it, Mom. Just call me the poop patrol!

"Where is Tailspin?"

I look around the room and call him. Slowly, a little nose sticks out from behind the couch. Then two ears and two paws. Then two more paws and a tail. It isn't spinning. It isn't even wagging.

"Tailspin!" I say in my strictest voice. Sort of like how Mrs. Green says "Eric!" after he's thrown a spitball.

The tail disappears behind the couch. Then the paws and then the ears, until only the nose is sticking out.

"Tailspin, come here," I say.

He slowly crawls forward, but I can't help smiling.

CHAPTER 7
A SPIN AROUND THE BLOCK

SO EXCITED →

I also have other duties. Taking Tailspin for a daily walk is one of them.

Actually, it is fun. When he sees his leash, he goes bananas! He jumps up and down and spins at the same time. When his leash is finally on, we head for the door. Well, Tailspin heads for the door and I am pulled along.

  ←BANANAS

Once we're out of the house, he wants to see everything. He tries to head in every direction at the same time. Now I'm the one spinning!

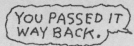

CHAPTER 8
TEACHING OLD TRICKS TO A NEW DOG

I've been trying to teach him some tricks without much luck. He's an independent thinker.

When I say "Stay," he comes.
When I say "Sit," he jumps.
When I say "Jump," he sits.

But he really is very smart. When he hears the crunch of a cookie or the rustle of a candy wrapper, he comes and jumps and sits. Food has a magic effect on him. His nose knows.

← COOKIE

He'll sit for hours by the dinner table looking up like he's starving, even though he just finished off a whole bowl of dog food.

I don't know how he can eat so much. He's not much bigger than the bowl.

CRUNCH
CRUNCH
CRUNCH

I try to ignore him and eat my dinner, but he makes me feel guilty with every forkful.

Mom says not to spoil him, but I always sneak him a little snack. That's just what best friends do.

FROG TREAT→

CHAPTER 9
THE BATH

Tomorrow is Show and Tell in my class.

Mom says if I don't want it to be "Show and Smell," I need to give Tailspin a bath. She says she'll help me.

We fill the tub halfway and pick up Tailspin. At first, he doesn't want to go in. I guess he's not part Water Spaniel. But finally I lower him in.

Mom pours some shampoo over him and he disappears in bubbles. We gently scrub him. I think he likes baths even less than I do.

After a good washing, Tailspin jumps out of the tub and shakes water all over the bathroom.

We get a big towel and throw
it over him. When he's dry, Mom
and I brush him. Now he looks
like a fancy show dog. I hope he
doesn't run around the backyard
and roll in the dirt until after Show
and Tell is over.

CHAPTER 10
SHOW AND TELL DOG

It's finally Friday, which means I get to bring Tailspin to school with me.

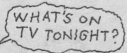

50

He is all bright and clean. In fact, his fur sparkles. He is ready to go.

Mom drives us to school and Tailspin's tail is in high gear. When we get there, all the kids crowd around us to pet him. He is a superstar. The class turtle and

goldfish are totally ignored. No one wants to pet them. Everyone wants to pet Tailspin, even Mrs. Green. She picks us to go first.

OH, MY, LOOK AT THAT CUTE PUPPY.

CHAPTER 11

I CAN'T SAY ENOUGH

I tell the class all about him. How smart he is. How he's learning to chase a ball and fetch a stick. How he has made friends with

every dog on our block, but not
the cats. He tries, but they are
not as friendly as dogs. Penny's
cat hisses just to prove my point.

I tell them how he sits on my lap and I read to him. We're reading *Lassie Come Home*, and he can't wait to see how it ends.

It's a wonderful day at school. At recess everyone wants to play with him, and at lunchtime everybody wants to feed him.

 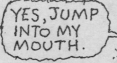 

Mrs. Green asks Tailspin if he will be in our class play. He eagerly wags his tail, and Penny's cat, who's jealous, hisses.

CHAPTER 12
A STAR IS BORN

All weekend Tailspin practices his lines.

"Bark!"

"Woof!"

And by Monday, he's ready.

He was born for the stage. He steals the show. He sniffs all the paper flowers and chews on a cardboard tree.

He gets a standing ovation and I swear he bows. He's going to be hard to live with now.

CHAPTER 13
FRIENDS FOREVER

When we get home, he goes out in the backyard and rolls in the dirt. He's the same old Tailspin, my best friend!

63

That night he lies at the foot of my bed and dreams about his wonderful day at school. And I dream about all the wonderful new adventures we are going to have together.